Tommy and the T-Tops

Helping Children Overcome Prejudice

Frederick Alimonti and Ann Tedesco, Ph.D.

Illustrations by John Hazard

New Horizon Press
Far Hills, NJ

Dedication

To Simone, Celeste and Lucas...

With love,

Mom and Dad

New Horizon Press
P.O. Box 669
Far Hills, NJ 07931

Alimonti, Frederick and Tedesco, Ann Ph.D.
Illustrations by Hazard, John
Tommy and the T-Tops: *Helping Children Overcome Prejudice*

Cover Design: Ron Hart with Robert Aulicino
Interior Design: Ron Hart

Library of Congress Control Number: 2007936342

ISBN 13: 978-0-88282-305-8
ISBN 10: 0-88282-305-1

SMALL HORIZONS
A Division of New Horizon Press

2013   2012   2011   2010   2009   /   5   4   3   2   1

Printed in the U.S.A.

It was another hot day by the
lake. Three-year-old Tommy the Triceratops stood near his mother,
basking in the sun.

Like the rest of his family and his whole herd, Tommy was a
vegetarian. He ate nothing but plants. They visited the same lake this
time every year because of its lush vegitation. The water was always cool
and refreshing.

All around him were other dinosaurs of his herd—triceratops, "T-Tops" for short. Like them, Tommy had different shades of green on his body and skin. When he went into the shade of the green forest, he almost seemed to disappear. This helped him to hide from meat-eating dinosaurs like Tyrannosaurus Rex.

There were about 300 dinosaurs in Tommy's herd. They were led by Thor, a giant male, or "bull". Thor had been leader since he fought Alexander and won.

Alexander stayed with the herd after his fight with Thor. He had become a friend of Tommy's. He was very wise.

One day, Tommy asked Alexander, "How did it feel when you lost the fight with Thor, and he became the new leader?"

"My, that's a big question for a young dinosaur." Alexander paused for a moment and then grinned.

"Tommy, I have been very lucky," he proclaimed. "For more than twenty years, I led this herd. I saw it nearly double in size."

"Do you miss it—being a leader and all?" Tommy asked.

"Sometimes a little," Alexander sighed. "Nothing can last forever. When I was a leader, I did the best I could for the herd—trying to lead it in good times and bad. Then Thor won his challenge and I turned the herd over to him. Now it is his turn to lead and learn."

"Well, I like you, Alexander," Tommy smiled. "You can be my leader any day. I think you're cool."

"Why, thank you, Thomas," Alexander replied as he gently prodded Tommy with his nose spike. "Now, go play with the other young pups."

Tommy headed toward the center of the herd where the children gathered to play. A wall of grown-ups were around them. One of the laws of the herd was that no dinosaur pup was to leave the herd. Ever! No adult would let a child get lost or left behind if he or she could help it.

A few days later, as the herd was gathered at the watering hole. Out of the woods a short distance from them emerged three dinosaurs, two grown-ups and a child about Tommy's size. They had stripes—black and orange stripes.

Thor made his way to the front of the herd at the water's edge. Everyone moved aside to let the leader pass.
"This is our water! Get out!" Thor roared. "This lake belongs to the green dinosaurs."

The striped dinosaurs kept drinking. The big striped bull, who was almost as large as all three of the bulls, turned toward them and charged straight at Thor. The striped female and child T-Tops quickly ran away as Thor fell backwards. Many of the dinosaurs from Tommy's herd chased after them and called them names.

After chasing the three striped dinosaurs a short distance, Tommy and the other T-Tops returned to the lake. Tommy was so excited. He rushed over to Alexander to tell him what had happened.

"We chased those three strange dinosaurs away from the lake. I bet they'll never come back here again!" Tommy exclaimed.

"That's too bad," said Alexander. "It might have been very interesting to talk to them."

"Why?" Tommy asked.

"Well, I've seen dinosaurs of all shapes and sizes—all species, too," Alexander explained. "All of them have different tools that suit them. Our green colors help us to hide in the forest from the T-Rex. Those dinosaurs had stripes. I wonder where they came from, what they could teach us. Most important, I wonder why there were just three of them. Where is their herd?"

A moment ago, Tommy had felt proud of helping the herd. Now he felt sad.

The next day, Tommy and his friend Billy were playing hide and seek when Billy said, "Tommy, let's sneak away. Let's try to find the striped dinosaurs. Then we can report back to Thor. We'll be scouts!"

"The herd will never let us go alone," Tommy replied. "They are always watching us. It's like having 200 mothers."

"Yeah, but I have a plan," Billy replied. "Look over there."

He pointed to a giant tree that had fallen into the lake. Its branches and leaves reached into the air, blocking anything behind it.

"We can wade into the lake for a drink," Billy said. "Then we hold our breath and slip under the tree. Once we're on the other side of it, no one will be able to see us sneak into the forest."

"What if we get lost?" Tommy asked. "What if they notice we're missing and start looking for us?"

"We'll be back before dark," Billy laughed. "Once we tell Thor about the striped dinosaurs, we'll be heroes."

The two young dinosaurs waded into the lake, slipped under the tree and began their search.

Tommy and Billy walked deeper into the woods, looking for three sets of tracks from three T-Tops. Finally, they passed through a muddy area with three clear sets of prints. They followed the tracks to a small stream. Tired, Tommy and Billy stopped for a drink.

Suddenly, there was a loud crash behind them. Bounding out of the woods was a T-Rex—a giant one. Before they knew it, he was inches away from them. The T-Rex snapped at Billy with his huge jaws and six-inch fangs. He barely missed. Tommy charged at the T-Rex's right leg. The small T-Tops smashed into the giant T-Rex and for a moment, the T-Rex fell. Tommy and Billy ran as fast as they could. As they raced up the hill, a big rock blocked their path. Creeping around it, they found the opening to a shallow cave in the rock and the two pups hid inside.

The T-Rex ran towards them. His huge head stretched inside the cave. The T-Rex's sharp teeth were inches away. The two T-Tops backed up to the cave wall, shivering in fear.

Suddenly, the T-Rex let out the loudest roar they had ever heard and fell down in front of the cave.

Then a voice from outside the cave shouted, "Run, children! Run! Get away from here!"

"Let's get out of here, Tommy!" Billy shouted. The two young dinosaurs darted out of the cave. Billy began running, but Tommy stopped and hid behind a log to see what happened to the T-Rex.

T-Rex got back on his feet, ready to pounce. Tommy saw the striped T-Top—the same one who had knocked over Thor at the lake. Stripe backed up and leaped at T-Rex, who turned and ran away into the woods.

"Thank you, sir," Tommy replied, climbing over the log.

Stripe nodded. "What is your name?"

"Tommy, and that's Billy over there," Tommy answered, pointing at Billy as he walked towards them.

"Hello boys. My name is Hector. It's nice to meet you. Why have you left your herd? Our young dinosaurs have to stay with the adults."

"We snuck away," admitted Billy.

"Snuck away? Why would you do that?"

"To find you guys," Tommy replied.

"You and your friend could have been badly hurt," Hector warned.

"I know. I'm sorry," Tommy frowned. "Hector, why did you help us? Don't you know we are from the herd that chased you away from the water?"

"Of course I do," Hector said. "However, in our herd, we all protect our young dinosaurs. The young are everyone's children."

Hector added, "Yesterday, you and your herd chased us away from the water. Today, you have become my friend." Hector looked at Tommy and Billy kindly.

"I think you pups have learned something very important," Hector proclaimed. "We should not be afraid of others who look or seem different."

Tommy thought about what Hector said. "Yes, I agree!"

"Well then, let's get you back to your herd." Hector called, "Family, come out, we're going for a walk."

His wife, Beth, who was expecting a baby very soon and their child, Fred, emerged from the forest. The five of them headed for the lake. For the first time in their history, a striped triceratops and a green triceratops walked side by side as friends.

"Where are you from?" Tommy asked the striped dinosaurs as they continued walking back to the green herd.

"From the grasslands," replied Hector. "Where we come from, there are miles of grassy plains and it is some of the tastiest grass you could ever imagine. We were sorry to leave it, but we had no choice."

"Why did you leave?" asked Tommy.

"The war," answered Hector.

"War? What is that?" Tommy responded.

"It's a terrible thing," Beth replied. "Hundreds of dinosaurs died in it."

"How did it happen?" Tommy asked.

"It started with the drought," Hector answered. "Slowly, the drinking waters began to dry up. Waters began to trickle and disappear. Finally, there were just a few places left to drink. The dinosaurs began fighting each other so they could claim the waters. Our herd fought another herd of T-Tops over the same watering hole for years."

"You mean the drought lasted that long?"

"No, Tommy. It ended years ago. By that time, all they knew was fighting each other. The war continued."

"Why did you leave?" Tommy asked.

"We could never survive long out here, just the three of us," Hector stated. We need a herd to protect us. Beth is going to have a baby. We need to be part of a herd, part of a bigger family."

"Wow!" exclaimed Tommy. "Will your baby have stripes, too?"

"It surely will," Beth replied.

"Those stripes," Tommy said. "They help you hide in the tall grass like our green shades help us hide in the forest, don't they?"

"Why yes, Tommy," answered Beth.

Tommy, Billy and their new friends came to the lake where they had first seen the striped T-Tops. Suddenly, they saw Thor and the other bulls. Thor recognized the striped male and he wanted to fight.

"Well, it's you three again!" Thor roared. "This time, you won't be able to run away."

"Get them," Thor ordered the other bulls. Dozens of bulls surrounded the three dinosaurs and Tommy.

"Clear out, Tommy. We'll take care of you. You're back with your herd now," some of the other bulls shouted.

"No!" Tommy yelled. "Hector saved Billy and me. He saved us from T-Rex."

Thor ignored Tommy. He lowered his head, preparing to charge Hector. The circle of dinosaurs drew closer and tighter around Tommy and his friends.

Thor charged at Hector. Hector smoothly stepped aside and Thor crashed past him into the bulls of his own herd. That made Thor even angrier. Thor turned, planted his feet to make another lunge at Hector. When he looked up, Alexander had stepped into the circle. He now stood between Thor and Hector.

Thor charged at Alexander. Alexander jumped aside just as he had seen Hector do moments before. Only this time, instead of running into his own herd, Thor ran straight into Hector's horns and snout. The horns only struck his armor collar and Thor's wounds were slight.

As Thor backed away from Hector, Alexander whispered in his ear. "Thor, now is your chance to really lead. Show these dinosaurs some mercy. Talk to them. Put aside your pride and your anger, so we can all learn something."

Thor thought hard about what Alexander had said and let down his guard. Hector did the same.

"That's enough fighting for today," Thor ordered. "You have saved these pups for us and I think we should thank you, not fight you."

"Yes!" Tommy shouted.